First published in Great Britain in 2011 by Andersen Press Ltd.,
20 Vauxhall Bridge Road, London SW1V 2SA.
Published in Australia by Random House Australia Pty.,
Level 3, 100 Pacific Highway, North Sydney, NSW 2060.
Colour separated in Switzerland by Photolitho AG, Zürich.
Printed and bound in China by C & C Offset Printing.
Tony Ross has used ink, pen and watercolour in this book.
10   9   8   7   6   5   4   3   2   1
British Library Cataloguing in Publication Data available.
ISBN 978 1 84939 250 1

STICKY ENDS

JEANNE WILLIS   TONY ROSS

ANDERSEN PRESS

For Gay Bridgewood,
for thirty years of titters and chortles. J.W.

To my dear mum and dad –
they always thought that I would come to one. T. R.

Contents

Guess What I Had for School Dinner?

monday

Guess what I had for school dinner?
They said it was Egg and Cheese Pie,
But I found a tooth in the pastry
And one of my mates found an eye.

Tuesday

Guess what I had for school dinner?
They said it was Toad-in-the-hole,
But I knew the cook was a liar
When I found a frog in my bowl.

Wednesday

Guess what I had for school dinner?
They said it was Dumplings and Stew,
It's odd because Stuart's gone missing
And so have the Dumpling Twins too.

Thursday

Guess what I had for school dinner?
They called it Sultana Surprise,
For there was no fruit in my custard
Just hundreds of fat little flies.

Friday

Guess what I had for school dinner?
I didn't have any at all,
From now on, I'll bring in a sandwich
And eat my packed lunch in the hall . . . eugh!

Squiggle McSquirm

Squiggle McSquirm was a toffee-nosed worm,
Who hatched in a compost heap,
He slithered away on a cabbage leaf sleigh
When his mother was fast asleep.

"The compost is damp. It is giving me cramp,"
Niggled Squiggle. "It's smelly and dark,
I need my own flat, I'd be happy with that
Or a house with a view of the park."

He went for a drink and a bit of a think
About where he should go for the best
When a funny old bird said, "You're homeless, I've heard."
And invited him back to her nest.

She wooed him with news of its wonderful views
And suggested he stayed for a week,
And as there was neither a staircase or lift,
She would carry him up in her beak.

"This is a giggle," thought silly McSquiggle,
"This is a riot!" he said,
The bird remained quiet and thought of her diet:
A worm between slices of bread.

"I wish I had butter," he heard the bird mutter,
"B . . . butter?" he stuttered. "Why so?"
It all became clear and squirming with fear
He leapt for the gutter below.

He turned very pale, "She has swallowed my tail!
Oh, how I wish I were dead!"
"There's no need to wail," said a wandering snail,
"At least you kept hold of your head."

He missed his old heap; it was safe, it was deep
And although as homes go, it was rotten,
To him it was nice, it was worm paradise
Something Squiggle had sadly forgotten.

He wormed his way in with a whoop and a grin
And his kith and his kin threw him parties,
For now he knew Happiness lived down below
And that home is the heap where your heart is.

Bubblegum Pete

This is the story of Bubblegum Pete
Who ate all the bubblegum he could eat.
There was gum in his pockets and gum in his boots
Gum in his socks and his shorts and his suits.

Sticky pink lumps, sometimes wrapped, often not
Wherever he went to, the bubblegum got.
And when he had finished this mess of a sweet
He would spit it and stick it on somebody's seat.

"Please don't chew gum, you are sure to get wind,"
His mother asked kindly, but Peter just grinned.
But wind as it happened did give him some trouble
When Pete blew the world's biggest bubblegum bubble.

He was out in the garden with nothing to do
So he put in some gum and he started to chew
When it went mushy he started to blow
And little by little it started to grow,

As big as a golf ball, as big as a mouse,
As big as a horse then as big as a house.
The giant gum bubble was caught by a breeze
Which wafted poor Peter up over the trees,

Higher and higher right over the steeple
Higher until he could not see the people,
Up in the clouds like some rare sort of bird
Where silly boys crying for help can't be heard.

Higher than spaceships and higher than stars
Higher than Venus and Saturn and Mars.
"I will never blow bubbles again. I will stop,"
Said Peter quite rightly. The bubble went

POP!

Felicity Finch

Felicity Finch was prone to pinch
Her little friends at nursery,
No matter what the teacher said
She went from bad to worsery.
They forced her into knitted mitts
And hoped that it would foil her
But she bit the mittens off
And threw them in the boiler.

Felicity Finch made infants flinch
And there was no excusing it,
She'd sneak up on the nearest knee
And take delight in bruising it.
She'd grab a chubby chunk of flab
And twist it with her thumbery
And woe betide them when she pinched
Her victims on the bummery.

Felicity Finch gave not an inch,
Her fingers gripped like pliers
If any of the kids complained
She called them freaks and liars.
She even tweaked the choir boys
While they were in rehearsary;
She was the cruellest of nippers
In the universery.

Felicity Finch said, "It's a synch
To pinch and I shan't stop it!"
Despite the pleas to please desist
Young Fliss refused to drop it.
So you'll be very glad to hear
That on a trip to Italy
The waiter brought a plate of lobster
Garnished very prettily.

But when she bent to take a bite
The lobster gripped her nosery
And did he ever let it go?
Well, what do you supposery?
He nipped it off, snip snippy snip
And did a victory dancery
And jumped into the sea with it
And took it home to Francery.

I Lost My Teddy

I lost my teddy in the woods
When I was only three,
I went alone to find him
But wherever could he be?

I called his little teddy name
And searched among the trees
And there behind a bush
I saw his furry teddy knees.

I grabbed his little teddy paw
And ran away from there,
Alas, it wasn't Teddy...
Just a very angry bear!

The Tale of Icy Clare

Oh, hear the tale of Icy Clare,
Who ran off in her underwear
When Mother tried to get her dressed
Beyond her frilly pants and vest.

What brought about this sudden dash?
It seems it was a fashion clash
Which rumbled on for many years,
Reducing both of them to tears.

For they could never quite agree
On how a girl should dress for tea
Or at a funeral or wake –
(Not as a ghost for goodness sake!)

Let's say her mother chose a hat;
Clare hollered, "I'm not wearing that!
You'll have to pin me to the bed
And nail the bonnet on my head!"

As tempting as this might have been,
It would have caused a frightful scene
With Social Services, no doubt,
So Mother let her scream and shout

About the choice of frocks and shoes,
If Clare was not allowed to choose
She'd kick up an enormous stink;
"I *won't* wear bows! I *won't* wear pink!"

Though Mother was a feisty foe
Exhausted, she would let her go
To certain places, unattired
In the proper clothes required,

As if it was the fashion to
Wear tights and tutu to the zoo,
And wellingtons to ballet school,
And trousers in the swimming pool.

Her little daughter got her way
Until one sad December day
When Mother felt, with proper reason,
That her clothes should suit the season.

So when Clare saw flakes of snow
And most excited, begged to go
Outside at once, so she could play
Her wretched mother made her stay

Until she dressed from head to toe
Just like a little Eskimo.
Despite the fact her daughter hated
Being over-insulated,

Mother made her wear six jumpers
And some ski boots (real clumpers!)
Several pairs of socks, a muff
And lots of other woolly stuff,

She even used the itchy cladding
From the loft as extra padding,
Fully clothed against the cold
She could go out, the child was told.

But little Clare had other plans,
She shook the mittens from her hands
As soon as she was out of view
And kicked the clumpy boots off too.

Took off her hat and with a laugh
Removed her socks and coat and scarf,
Her jumpers and her dungarees
And danced around with naked knees

Oblivious to ice and snow –
Until it fell to four below.
Then darkness came. A blizzard blew
Her pile of clothing out of view

And when she went to put them on
She searched in vain for they had gone.
Likewise, her parents looked for her
Alas, the landscape was a blur,

There was no little girl to see;

Just drifts of snow. Where could she be?

They searched but never found a thing,

Except a snowman on her swing.

If only it had melted there;

That was no snowman . . .

. . . That was Clare.

Vince the Mince

Vince the Mince, Vince the Mince, prince of the butcher's yard,
I've never seen a butcher's dog who looks so mean and hard.
His head is like a lump of lead, his eyes are glowing coals
His growl is like a grizzly bear's, his ears are full of holes.
His face is scarred and scabby and his mouth is full of knives
When they see him, thugs and thieves are frightened for their lives.

Vince the Mince, Vince the Mince, the greatest guard dog yet!
He doesn't like the vicar and he cannot stand the vet.
He really hates the dustman, I am quite convinced of that
And he did a most disgusting thing to Mister Postman's hat.
They say he eats policemen, but I can't believe it's true
But I did find something sticky in his kennel, which was blue.

Vince the Mince, Vince the Mince! His collar's full of spikes,
He likes to chase articulated lorries, planes and bikes;
And when I take him walkies on his massive metal chain
Villains run off screaming and are never seen again.

Vince the Mince, Vince the Mince, he guards the butcher's gates
He has a little secret, but you mustn't tell your mates.
My dad says it's embarrassing; that's why he's up for sale,
I can tell he really likes you by the way he wags his tail.

32

I'm begging you to take him. See, he wants to be your friend!
A gentle word of warning; a refusal may offend.
I really hate to part with him, but Dad says he must go.
The reason is – don't laugh – he's vegetarian, you know.

As a butcher's son I find it hard to understand
Why Vince loves peas and carrots but he eats them from my hand.
He loves a bit of cabbage and he's very fond of swedes,
But he won't touch bones or brisket, beef or anything that bleeds.

That business with the postman's hat? Vince wasn't after him,
He just ate the beetroot sarny that was tucked inside the brim.
That blue thing in his kennel? No, he hadn't killed a cop;
He'd pinched a bag of plums from some old biddy in a shop.

Dad calls Vince a chicken, but I'm telling you, he ain't!
He's very sensitive, that's all, and liver makes him faint.
He hates the smell of sausages; they really make him heave
So I sneak him bits of celery I've hidden up my sleeve.

Now Dad has caught us at it and he says it's bad for trade,
The greengrocer came round today demanding to be paid
For all the fruit and vegetables I pinched for Vince to eat;
Dad says our dog has got to go unless he sticks to meat.

So, go on, find it in your heart to give a home to Vince,
He's very fond of raspberries but you must give them a rinse.
He's just a great big softy and he wouldn't hurt a fly,
Unless you overcook his sprouts. In which case, you will . . .

. . . DIE!!!

Sorry, Father Christmas

Sorry, Father Christmas
But I'm feeling very sad.
I don't suppose you'll come tonight
Because I've been so bad.

I didn't really clean my teeth
Although I said I did.
I wet my toothbrush, spat
And just unscrewed the toothpaste lid.

I never ate my vegetables,
I hid them in my shoe.
I'm scared your elves will snitch on me;
My sisters always do.

But that's not all; the other day
I pulled my cousin's hair.
And I left my chewing gum
On Grandpa's rocking chair.

At school, I put a little frog
Down Daisy Dingle's shirt.
I can't think why she yelled so much;
It wasn't like it hurt.

I also broke the window;
I was playing in the yard
But how was I supposed to know
My conker was so hard?

I let my mouse out in the church
When Auntie May got wed.
At least I didn't say rude words;
Not like the bridesmaid said.

I'm sorry I ate all the cake
My mother baked for Nan.
I'm sorry that my fizzy drink
Got shook up in the can.

I'm sorry that I pushed my brother
Too high on the swing.
But how was that my fault?
He should have held on to the thing!

And when I shut Mum in the shed,
Well, that was a mistake.
She hardly ever goes in there,
Why now for heaven's sake?

Oh dear, Father Christmas
I have done some dreadful stuff
I've tried to say I'm sorry
But I bet it's not enough.

I really wouldn't blame you
If you didn't bring me toys
And gave them to those goody-goody
Little girls and boys.

But before you make your mind up,
There is something you should know;
I saw you here last Christmas Eve,
You came in from the snow.

You made yourself a sandwich
And you helped yourself to beer
And ate the plate of carrots
That I put out for your deer.

Then you watched our telly
And you ate our nuts and dates
Then you used our telephone
To call up all your mates.

Then you used our toilet
And I know that it was you
Because you left the seat up
Which my dad would never do.

I took your photo, Father Christmas
On my mobile phone,
I may have been a naughty boy,
It seems I'm not alone!

But if you leave some presents,
I won't tell a soul, I swear . . .
I think you'll find my stocking
By the chimney over there!

My Uncle's Wedding

My uncle married a monkey
We called her Aunt Baboon,
We all went to their wedding
In the merry month of June.

The bridesmaid was a gibbon,
The page boy was a goat,
The best man, a gorilla who
Got grandpa by the throat.

The vicar was a rhino
And this was a mistake;
He charged the congregation and
He tossed the wedding cake.

The guests behaved like animals
And trashed the hotel room
But sad to say the worst behaved
Was Uncle George, the groom.

Lardy Marge

Lardy Marge was rather large
The reason, so they said
Was that she buttered everything
Beyond the buns and bread.

She buttered crisps, she buttered cake
She spread it on her chips,
She put butter on her cornflakes
And her hands and knees and lips.

"Marge, put down the butter knife
And throw the dish away,
You'll turn into a butter pat!"
Her aunt said in dismay.

Too late, for Marge turned yellow
From her head down to her feet.
She went to play out in the sun
And melted in the street.

The moral of the story is
Go easy on the fat,
Or just like Marge, you'll melt
And you'll be licked up by the cat.

Some Short Ones from the Swamp

Alligator sits in the swamp and waits
With his knife and his fork and his dinner plates
Until his lunch comes walking by;
Little Girl Pudding and Little Boy Pie.

Doctor Livingstone went to explore,
He was one of the bravest sorts
But he was as scared as a man can be
When a snake shot up his shorts!

Quicksand's not like seaside sand
It sucks you down, down, down,
So walk around it, if you please
Unless you want to drown.

Don't swim in the river Zambesi
Who knows what is lurking in there?
A python may squeeze you
Or monkeys may tease you
And steal your underwear.

Elephants Do Not Forget

An elephant does not forget
Or so the experts say,
So if you have been rude to one
Then keep out of its way.
For if you said its bum was big
It would not stand for that,
Quite rightly it would sit down hard
Upon your Sunday hat.

The Boy Who Knew Best

There once was a boy, I am sorry to say
Who insisted on having it all his own way,
Which was all very well if he knew what to do
But this little Know-It-All hadn't a clue.
The worst of it was, he believed that he did;
No wonder his friends called him Silly the Kid.

He just wouldn't listen to any advice
He did as he pleased and he didn't think twice.
If his mother suggested he tied up the lace
On his trainers, in case he fell flat on his face
He ignored her completely and went into town.
Of course he tripped over! Of course he fell down!

Did he learn? Did he heck! He just grinned like a cat
And announced to the world that he meant to do that.
If his father suggested he'd poke out an eye
If he ran with the scissors, he'd only reply
That the scissors were blunt and that he didn't mind
If he slipped with the blade and was registered blind.

Did he slip? Yes, he did and got more than a scratch
But he claimed he liked pirates and wanted a patch.
And if on a zoo trip his granny suggested
That creatures like tigers should not be molested,
He'd say she knew nothing and fly in a rage
And to prove it, he'd stick both his hands in the cage.

Did he lose all his fingers? Yes, all except one
Which he pointed at Granny and said it was fun
Because now that he couldn't hold onto a pen
He'd never be asked to do homework again.

And if, by a cliff it said, "Keep Off The Edge."
He would instantly head for the crumbliest ledge
Because he knew better and balanced so well.
Could he heck! Did he fall? Yes, he jolly well fell.
And what did he say when he shattered his spine?
"I love it in hospital! Really, I'm fine."

He just wouldn't learn. If the lights were on red
He assumed it was best to go full speed ahead
If it said, "Do not skate." He would take no advice
And grandly he'd stand on the thinnest of ice.
"NO TRESPASSING," meant that he had to explore,
"NO ENTRY"? The silly lad went through the door
And there was a button which said, "DO NOT PRESS."

And what did he do? Well, I think you can guess . . .
He fired a rocket which started a war,
Why did he do it? What reason, what for?
As the world blew to pieces, he puffed out his chest
And he said with a smile, "It's because I know best."

The Tale of Filthy Frankie

Hear the fate of Filthy Frankie
Who refused to use a hanky.
Even though his father told him
And his mother used to scold him

Frequently upon the issue,
"Frankie, you must use a tissue!"
He ignored them! In despair
They caught him sneezing in the air

And spreading snot and germs like butter
With a snort and with a splutter.
"Frances, use your hanky, please!"
They said, "Or you will spread disease."

But frankly, Frankie didn't care
He picked his nostrils anywhere
And rooted round his runny nose
With fingers, sticks and spoons and toes.

And horrid though it is, I'm certain
That he used his grandma's curtain
As a wiper for his snout,
And her tablecloth, no doubt

But like all boys who don't give tuppence
Filthy Frank got his comeuppance
When he stole his Grandpa's snuff
And he inhaled the wretched stuff.

Not just a pinch, but half a pot
And goodness, did he sneeze a lot!
He sneezed so hard the strings of goo
Shot from his nose like superglue

And wrapped around his head and face
Like grotty, snotty sticky lace

And as his pocket had no hanky

It set hard on little Frankie

And too late to wipe it off, he . . .

Turned into a human toffee.

Shunned by family and friends

His was the stickiest of ends

But rather sweet if it achieves

A handkerchief up certain sleeves.

Spec-Less Rex

Oh, hear the tale of Feckless Rex
Who would not wear his reading specs
Despite the fact he couldn't tell
"D" from "G" or "I" from "L".
And mixed his Q's with P's and O's
Though they were inches from his nose.

Despite the fact he chose the frames
From hundreds of designer names,
(The most expensive he could find)
His mother said she didn't mind
If Rex would wear them without fuss
And never leave them on the bus.

He promised – ah, but Feckless Rex
Just liked to watch her signing cheques
On his behalf and feeling clever
Vowed to never wear them – ever!

Stamped on them and with a grin
He threw them in the nearest bin
Whilst on the way to catch the train
To school, and waited in the rain.

A train arrived at Rex's station
And he read the destination
On the front and climbed aboard
But dear, oh dear, oh dear, oh Lord,
Of course he hadn't read it right
And I'm afraid to Rex's fright . . .

The train was not the School Express
He had mistaken "G" for "S"
And several other letters too,
(He had confused the "C" and "OO".)
Now had he worn his specs, the fool
He would have read that it said "Ghoul"
Not "School Express" which would explain
Why all the people on the train
Were ghosts and skeletons and hags
And zombies dressed in filthy rags
And as the train went underground
It just went round and round and round
And round the everlasting track;
Alas, there was no going back
And Feckless Rex missed all his classes
So be warned and wear your glasses!

Moaning Marty

Moaning Marty joined the party
Full of doom and gloom,
Which is why by 7.30
He had cleared the room.

He cornered everyone in turn
And moaned about the spread,
"The sandwiches are dry," he sighed,
"The ham inside is dead!"

He warned them all against the prawns
And said they made him sick,
Then criticised the angle
Of his sausage on a stick.

"These chairs are far too hard," he said.
"The music's way too loud.
This room is cramped, it smells of damp,
I do not like this crowd."

He said the games were stupid
And was horrid to the host,
He would not say hip hip hooray
When friends proposed a toast.

And when the birthday cake was lit
And everybody sang,
He said he hated gateau,
And he spat out his meringue.

He ruined every photo
And refused to give a smile
He stamped on all the presents
And announced that they were vile.

He tore up all the birthday cards
And kicked them round the floor
And muttered, "What a load of poop!"
And pulled a face and swore.

At which point, everybody left;
They grabbed their coats and ran
So Marty's older sister
Pushed him face-first in a flan

For ruining her birthday
And for being such a bore
And that's why Marty doesn't go
To parties any more.

Don't Go to the Bathroom

Don't go to the bathroom at bedtime
With both your eyes shut tight,
No matter how weary you're feeling
You must snap on the light.

I have a sister who didn't
Who had the most awful mishap;
A monster was using the toilet and . . .
My sister sat down on his lap!

Never Give a Crocodile for Christmas

Never give a crocodile for Christmas,
Crocodiles are such a funny shape.
They're really hard to wrap,
They wriggle, bite and snap
No matter how much string you use
They're certain to escape.

Never give a crocodile for Christmas,
It's a crazy, crackers thing to do,
He'll hide behind the tree
And I am certain he
Will chew on Father Christmas
When he clambers down the flue.

Never give a crocodile for Christmas,
He'll gobble up the turkey off your plate
He'll swallow every dish,
The pudding and the wish,
And leave you with the parsnips
And the sprouts you really hate.

Never give a crocodile for Christmas,
Get your folk some chocolates or socks,
Or how about a game?
You'll only get the blame
If your darling little cousins
Are consumed by hungry crocs.

Never give a crocodile for Christmas,
Take it back and swap it straight away.
Perhaps a pet iguana?
Though I think that a piranha
Would be perfect for your sister
In the bath on Christmas Day!

I Found a Little Puppy

I found a little puppy dog,
His coat was soft and brown
He had two beady little eyes
That looked me up and down.
He had a funny little tail
I found him in a drain,

But Mother wasn't too impressed
And put him back again.
She screamed, "He is no puppy,
I am very sure of that!"
But I am sure she'll grow to love
My little sewer rat.